W9-AXU-192

Pond Walk

Written and illustrated by
Nancy Elizabeth Wallace

Marshall Cavendish Children

Have fun taking
Pond Walks!
your friend,
Nancy Elizabeth Wallace
2014

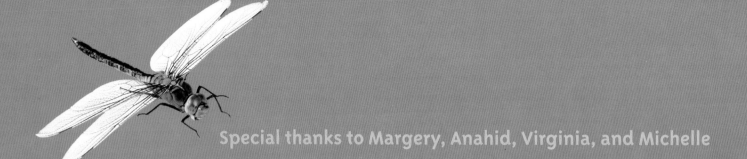

Special thanks to Margery, Anahid, Virginia, and Michelle

Text and illustrations copyright © 2011 by Nancy Elizabeth Wallace

Marshall Cavendish Corporation, 99 White Plains Road, Tarrytown, NY 10591
www.marshallcavendish.us./kids

Library of Congress Cataloging-in-Publication Data
Wallace, Nancy Elizabeth.
Pond walk / written and illustrated by Nancy Elizabeth Wallace. — 1st ed.
p. cm.
Summary: One summer day, Buddy and his mother take a walk around a pond and
observe the animals and insects that live there.
ISBN 978-0-7614-5816-6
[1. Pond animals—Fiction. 2. Pond ecology—Fiction. 3. Ponds—Fiction.] I. Title.
PZ7.W15875 Wal
[E]—dc22
2010025281

The illustrations are rendered in paper, photographs, and colored pencils.
Book design by Virginia Pope
Editor: Margery Cuyler

Printed in China (E)
First edition
1 3 5 6 4 2

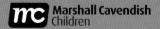

Marshall Cavendish
Children

For my Nature Buddies—
Cyd, Bobbi, and Claudia
Kate F. and Deb V.
Amy B. and Janet G.
Doe, Judy, Kay, Leslie B., Leslie C.,
Lorraine, and Mary-Kelly
Shaunee and Phil,
Diane and . . . Harvee,
and always for Peter and Mom
Love,
N.E.W.

Canary Yellow

Rose Red

One summer morning, Mama asked, "Would you like to go to Pete's Pond for a pond walk?"

"Yes!" said Buddy. "I like ponds! I hope I see a turtle!"

Mama parked the car near an old iron gate. They followed the path to Pete's Pond.

The sky was blue.

The warm summer air hummed with bug chatter.

A butterfly darted by.

Welcome to Pete's Freshwater Pond
Enjoy your visit!
— Pete

Ponds can become deep very quickly, so be careful!

Please respect all animals and plants.

Ducks and geese were making lots of noise. **QUACK. QUACK. QUACK.**
HONK. HONK. HONK.

Buddy called back, "Quack!
Quack! Honk! Honk!"

Black bugs were twirling
around and around on the
surface of the water.

"What are those?"
Buddy asked.

Mama got the field guide out of her backpack. "They are whirligig beetles," she said.

"Whirligig beetles!" said Buddy.

Mama read, "Whirligig beetles have eyes with two parts so they can see above and below the water at the same time."

Buddy took his drawing pad and colored pencils out of his backpack.

"Would you draw the eyes on my pad?" he asked.

They sat on the grass and drew.

Whirligig Beetle eyes
can see above
and below the
water

CROAK! CROAK!
"What's that?"
asked Buddy.

Buddy moved slowly toward the sound.
The croaking stopped.
He crouched down.
But what he saw hopped away.

Mama whispered, "What was it?"
Buddy drew a picture on his pad.
He showed it to her.

"A frog!" said Mama.
"Mama?" said Buddy.
"Yes, Bud."
"How did the frog feel when it hurt its leg?"
"How?" she asked.
"Very unHOPPY!"
They both giggled.
They walked along the edge of the pond.

frog

"Look, cattails," said Mama.

"The bump part looks like a hot dog on a stick," said Buddy.

"It does," said Mama. "The bump part is thousands of flowers pressed tightly together."

"Really?" asked Buddy.

"Yes," said Mama. "By the end of the summer, the bump will break apart. The flowers will have made seeds. The seeds will be scattered by the wind."

"It feels fuzzy . . . like a cat's tail!" said Buddy.

Buddy drew. He giggled. "Cattails!"

Then he saw some other plants.
Buddy got his magnifying glass out
of his backpack.

They waded over to look. "Green dots," said Buddy.
Mama found the plant in the field guide. "They're duckweed."
"Duckweed!" said Buddy.

Mama read, "Duckweed is a mass of tiny plants that grow really fast. They have floating roots. Strong wind can blow the plants around a pond."

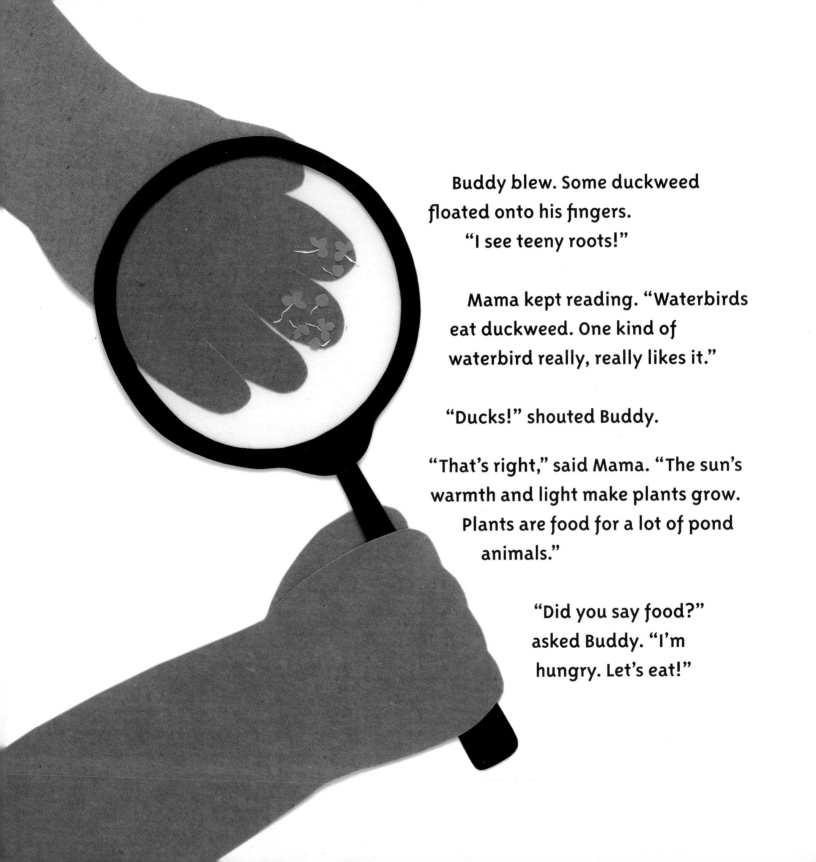

Buddy blew. Some duckweed floated onto his fingers. "I see teeny roots!"

Mama kept reading. "Waterbirds eat duckweed. One kind of waterbird really, really likes it."

"Ducks!" shouted Buddy.

"That's right," said Mama. "The sun's warmth and light make plants grow. Plants are food for a lot of pond animals."

"Did you say food?" asked Buddy. "I'm hungry. Let's eat!"

They found a bench and had a snack.

"Mama, what did the little duck want for its snack?"
"What?"
"Duckweed and quackers!"
They both laughed.
"Let's go find some more things," said Buddy.

They walked along and looked at the pond.

"Water lilies," said Mama.

"Their leaves are floating too!" said Buddy.

"But water lilies have roots that anchor them in the mud," said Mama. "And long underwater stems. When there's a lot of rain, the water in the pond rises, and the lily pads do too."

"Then I think that when the water goes down, the lily pads go down too," said Buddy.

"I think you are very smart," said Mama.

Suddenly Buddy stopped.

"Is that a dragonfly?"
Mama looked in the field guide.
"It's a damselfly."

Buddy held very still . . .

. . . until the damselfly flew away.

Mama read, "You can tell a dragonfly and a damselfly apart when they land.

Dragonflies land with their two pairs of wings outstretched."

Damselflies land with their two pairs of wings folded close to their bodies."

"Look!" said Buddy. "On the lily pad!"

"Lily pads make great landing pads for damselflies and dragonflies," said Mama. "And islands for frogs, and shade umbrellas for fish."

Buddy started drawing.

dragonfly

lily pad

Midnight Black

Grass Green

Rose Red

Mama read, "Dragonflies have big eyes that cover most of their head.

Their eyes allow them to see in all directions.

They can fly forward and backward.

They can stop and hover like a helicopter.

They can fly so fast, they can use their legs and feet to catch other flying insects to eat."

"Did you say eat?" asked Buddy. "I'm hungry!"

They spread a blanket on the grass and unpacked their picnic.

Buddy made the buns, celery, tomatoes, and carrot sticks into sandwich turtles.

Then he asked, "Mama? What kind of drawing pad do you use at the pond?"

"What kind?"

"A lily pad!"

Mama laughed.

After lunch Buddy picked up
a stick and drew in the dirt.

"I hope I see a real turtle."
"Let's go back to the edge of
the pond and keep looking,"
said Mama.

The pond bottom was mucky.
"I see pebbles. I see something
brown! It's moving!" shouted Buddy.
Mama yelled, "Scoop it up, quick!"

Buddy scooped.

"A salamander," said Mama.

"Look at its tiny front toes!" Buddy counted them. "Its skin is so soft. It's very wiggly." Buddy put the salamander back in the pond. "Back to your home."

"When a salamander walks, it spreads out its toes," said Mama.

"When a salamander swims, it pulls its toes together, like a fin," said Mama.

Buddy drew on his pad.

Salamander

"Do you
think there are
any turtles in this pond?"
he asked.

"There probably are," said Mama. "Let's look on tree
limbs that have fallen in the water and on the tops of rocks."

They packed up and walked on.

Buddy saw something. He stopped.
"Bugs zip, zip, zipping all around!"
"They're water striders," said Mama.
"The field guide says they are also called pond skaters."
Buddy watched them. "They have really long legs! I'm going to draw some pond skaters."

"How do they stay on top of the water?" he asked.
Mama read while Buddy drew. "They are very
light and skate on the water's surface."

They kept pond walking and looking for turtles.
"Turtles are reptiles," said Mama. "They can't make their own body heat so they sit in the sun to get warm. But they're skittish. They'll slip into the water faster than you can say . . ."
"Turtle!" said Buddy. "What do turtles eat?"

"I think they catch bugs for lunch and flies for dessert," said Mama.
"Did you say dessert?
Can we have another cookie?"
asked Buddy.

They climbed up on a big rock.

"Mama, why was the turtle a good baseball player?"
"Why?" asked Mama.
"Because he could catch flies!"
Mama laughed.

Buddy yawned. "A cloud turtle."

zzzzzzzzz zzzzzzzz zzzzzzzz zzzzzzzzz

"Tur . . .

. . . tle!"

"I saw a real turtle!"
Mama smiled.

"Nice art," said Mama. "Time to head on home, my young limnologist."

"Lim-nah-lo-gist. What's that?" asked Buddy. "Someone who likes to climb tree limbs?"

"A limnologist studies and learns about ponds," said Mama. "Just like you!"

As they walked back to the car, Buddy pointed.

"Mama! Look! A HUGE! . . . GIANT! . . ."

"TURTLE!"

shouted Buddy.

"WOW!" said Mama.

"I think this is the biggest turtle in the world!" said Buddy. "I want to make a rock turtle!"

"That's a super idea," said Mama.

And when they got home, Buddy did!

Buddy's Rock Turtle — You can make one too!

You will need: a small, smooth, turtle shell-shaped rock, paint, a thin paintbrush, a glue stick, scissors, and paper.

1. Paint the rock.

2. Cut the paper into shapes.

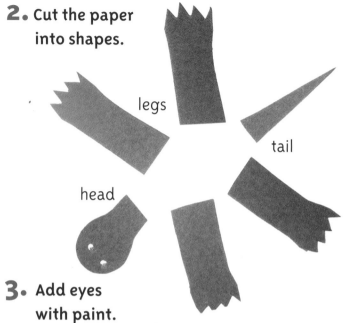

legs

tail

head

3. Add eyes with paint.

4. After the paint has dried, glue the head, tail, and legs onto the rock "shell."

You can make a paper pond for your turtle too.